This book of treasures belongs to

____

HIDDEN TREASURE

by

ELLY MACKAY

RP|KIDS
PHILADELPHIA

For treasure collectors: Lily, Koen, Phyllis, Ori & Eve

Running Press Kids
Hachette Book Group
1290 Avenue of the Americas, New York, NY 10104
www.runningpress.com/rpkids
@RP_Kids

Printed in China

First Edition: June 2021

Published by Running Press Kids, an imprint of Perseus Books, LLC, a subsidiary of Hachette Book Group, Inc. The Running Press Kids name and logo is a trademark of the Hachette Book Group.

Print book cover and interior design by Frances J. Soo Ping Chow.

Library of Congress Control Number: 2019946933

ISBNs: 978-0-7624-6301-5 (hardcover), 978-0-7624-6302-2 (ebook), 978-0-7624-7104-1 (ebook), 978-0-7624-7105-8 (ebook)

APS

10 9 8 7 6 5 4 3 2 1

I'm feeling lucky. How about you?
Do you want to search
for treasures, too?

Follow me. We'll go to the bay.
We'll pass the shops along the way.

THE
MERMAID
$10 each
TREASURE

They sell treasure here at the store.
But it's not the kind we're looking for.

In movies, treasure is always hidden—
pirate treasure, lost and forbidden.
But treasure is . . . everywhere.
You don't need a map to know it's there.

The beach stones sparkle in the dew.
Each time I come, there's something new.

See these treasures? Each has a tale.
This one looks like a tooth from a whale!

The water's cold, but here I go.
I spot a glimmer down below.

Three little shells and a speckled rock.
I line up my treasures on the dock.
A bubble wand, a rusty key,
a marble, too, all lost at sea.

Sometimes a treasure is too special to keep,
like cocoons where moths are fast asleep.

Some treasures won't come home with me,
but I'll always know where they'll be.

Now for the hardest part of my quest—
to choose the treasure I love the best.
This pink shell makes a whispering sound,
and this speckled stone is smooth and round.

Papa helps me pick from my pile
ones I can borrow, keep for a while.

I open up my treasure tin
and, carefully, I place them in.

When I'm here, I feel like a queen.
So I think I know what treasure means.

I love my rocks and feathers, too.
But what I treasure most . . .
is you.